# The Dog Who Loved to Race

*Other books in this series:*
The Cat Who Smelled Like Cabbage
The Hamster Who Got Himself Stuck
The Parrot Who Talked Too Much

Unless otherwise indicated, all Scripture references are from the Good News Bible, copyright American Bible Society, 1976.

Cover design by Durand Demlow
Illustrations by Anne Gavitt

THE DOG WHO LOVED TO RACE
© 1990 by Neta Jackson
Published by Multnomah Press
10209 SE Division Street
Portland, Oregon 97266

Multnomah Press is a ministry of Multnomah School of the Bible, 8435 NE Glisan Street, Portland, Oregon 97220.

Printed in Singapore.

**Library of Congress Cataloging-in-Publication Data**

Jackson, Neta.
    The dog who loved to race / Neta Jackson.
       p.  cm. —(Pet parables)
      Summary: A jealous puppy learns to share his best friend with others. Includes a Bible verse and discussion questions.
    ISBN 0-88070-350-4
    [1. Dogs—Fiction. 2. Jealousy—Fiction.  3. Parables.]
    I. Title. II Series: Jackson, Neta. Pet parables.
    PZ7.J13684Do   1990
    [E]—dc20                90-48383

                                                           CIP
                                                           AC

91 92 93 94 95 96 97 98 99 - 10 9 8 7 6 5 4 3 2 1

# The Dog Who Loved to Race

## Neta Jackson
### Illustrated by Anne Gavitt

MULTNOMAH
Portland, Oregon 97266

Pepper turned around in her bed under the kitchen counter and lay down with a "whumph." Her tummy felt tight and full after her good breakfast. Her Boy had mixed in juices from last night's pot roast with her regular dry food—he knew how much she loved beef juice. Ahh, time for a nice morning nap.

But just as Pepper contentedly closed her eyes, she heard a door open outside. Pepper's ears stood up. Yes, there was the familiar jangle of dog tags. Wolfie! Pepper spilled out of her bed, pushed open the screen door, and scrambled down the back steps. She halted at the wire fence and peered excitedly into the next yard. There was Wolfie, stretching himself on his People's back porch.

"Wolfie!" Pepper barked eagerly. "Let's race!"

Wolfie bounded over to the fence. Barely touching noses through the wire, both dogs took off along the fence, bodies low, legs stretching. At the end of the yard, Pepper slid to a stop, dust flying up into the sun, barked twice at Wolfie, then turned and raced back the other way. Wolfie raced beside her, his short legs pumping furiously to keep pace.

At the other end of the fence, the dogs barked furiously for one second, and turned back again. Pepper pulled ahead now, and by the time she got to the other end, Wolfie wasn't there. She looked back through the settling dust to see Wolfie flopped down in his yard.

"Come on, Wolfie, let's race again!" Pepper called.

Wolfie stretched his hind legs behind him, frog-like. "Nah," he yawned, "I want to sun a little."

Pepper stretched out in the little dirt path along the fence, tongue panting in a happy half-smile. It was always like this. A fast and furious race, then Wolfie giving up because Pepper always won. It really wasn't fair, because her legs were twice as long. Sometimes she wished he would win, just so she could keep on running. It didn't matter to her who won. She just loved to race.

The morning sun was warm, shining on her black fur. Pepper felt drowsy. If she waited a while longer, Wolfie would get his breath back, and maybe they could race again. . . .

Another door slammed and Pepper opened her eyes with a start. Wolfie was trotting away from her toward the fence on the other side of his yard, his tail stiff and unmoving. Pepper bounced up and peered hard through the fence. What did Wolfie see? Then she saw it, too: a strange dog. The dog was big and yellow, standing alert and still as Wolfie approached the far fence.

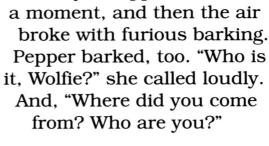

The short brown dog and the big yellow dog stood tensely on opposite sides for a moment, and then the air broke with furious barking. Pepper barked, too. "Who is it, Wolfie?" she called loudly. And, "Where did you come from? Who are you?"

Just then Pepper's Boy came out the back door. "Get in here, Pepper. You're making too much noise!"

Pepper hopped in her bed under the counter and curled up tightly. She could still hear Wolfie and the new dog barking. Then People voices and the barking stopped. She sighed and closed her eyes. Who was that dog?

Late that afternoon Pepper heard Wolfie's back door bang, and she hurried outside to the fence. The two dogs touched noses and the race was on! But in the middle of the race Pepper realized that Wolfie was gone. She stopped and looked. Wolfie was running over to his other fence. The big yellow dog was standing at the fence barking excitedly. Wolfie and the big yellow dog touched noses and began to race up and down the far fence.

Pepper rushed back and forth in distress. "Wolfie! Come back! Race with me!"

In a few minutes, Wolfie flopped down in his yard, panting.

"Who is that dog?" Pepper demanded. "Don't race with her. I want you to race with me."

Wolfie yawned. "She just moved in next door with her People. Her name is Goldie. She likes to play, too."

"But it's not fair!" scolded Pepper.

"Don't worry, Pepper," Wolfie soothed. "I like to play with you. You're my friend! Even if you do beat me all the time."

"Well," Pepper grumbled, "I'll even let you win if you just won't race with that new dog."

Wolfie just closed his eyes and panted in the sun.

But everything was changed. Wolfie still raced with Pepper if they were the only two dogs out in the yards. But if Goldie came out in her yard, off Wolfie would dash to touch noses and race with his new friend, too. Pepper scolded him when he returned to her fence. But Wolfie just shrugged and said, "Don't be so uptight, Pepper."

The next morning Pepper heard Wolfie bark for her. "Pepper! Come out and play!" Pepper started to get out of her bed—but on second thought she lay back down. "Why should I go race with Wolfie?" she grumbled to herself. "He'd rather race with Goldie, anyway. If she's not out there, he can just race with himself."

Sure enough, in a few minutes she heard Goldie's bark from the far yard. Well, let them have fun. She didn't care. They wouldn't even miss her.

Pepper lay in her bed and listened to Wolfie and Goldie barking and racing. Then the yards were quiet.

All that day Pepper sulked. She did not go outside when Wolfie was there. She went from room to room in the house, her nails clicking on the floor. She got up on the couch (when her People weren't looking) and watched the Boy play catch on the front sidewalk. She drank from her big crockery bowl. She lay on the cool floor with her head on her paws.

During her People's suppertime, Pepper went out into the back yard. The leaves on the maple tree were shaking gently in the breeze. Crickets were buzzing in the bushes. Pepper sniffed. It smelled like a good day, and she had missed it.

Then she saw Wolfie lying quietly in his yard, enjoying the evening. Pepper headed for the back steps. "Pepper, wait!" Wolfie barked, but she ignored him and gave a sharp bark at the screen door to be let in.

"Pepper, please come out and play," Wolfie called after her.

Pepper curled up in her bed under the kitchen counter and sighed. She didn't feel like another nap. She wanted to race. It was all Wolfie's fault. No, it was Goldie's fault. Everything was fine until Goldie moved in on the other side of Wolfie's yard.

Pepper wished she lived in Wolfie's yard. Then she could race whenever she wanted! She could race with Wolfie, and she could race with Goldie, too. "I wonder if I could beat Goldie?" Pepper mused. "She's bigger than I am. I'd have to run fast. But I bet I could beat her. Or maybe she would beat me. That would really be a race!"

Suddenly Pepper sat up. "If I lived in the middle yard, I would want to race with Goldie, too, just like Wolfie does!"

Just then Pepper heard a door bang and the jangle of dog tags. Sitting in the house was boring! She would just have to share Wolfie with the new yellow dog.

With an excited bark Pepper scrambled out the screen door and skidded to a stop by the fence. "C'mon, Wolfie, let's race!"

Wolfie answered by taking off for the back gate. Pepper raced alongside, only the fence and a whisker-length between them. Twice along the length of the yard. Race! Race! Race!

Just as Pepper pulled ahead, she heard Goldie's bark. Wolfie dashed off, and in a moment was racing Goldie along the far fence. Pepper stood at the fence and watched. Then suddenly she thought, "I'll race them, too!" She took off again, back and forth along her fence, keeping pace with the other two dogs on the other side of Wolfie's yard.

A three-way race! Pepper couldn't tell who won. It didn't matter. It just felt good to be racing with Wolfie again—and with Wolfie-and-Goldie, too.

*"Peace of mind makes the body healthy, but jealousy is like a cancer"* (Proverbs 14:30).

# To the Parent

Jealousy is no stranger to a child. How many toddlers have interrupted their parents' embrace with a demanding, "Me hug! Me hug!"? From tots to teens, when one's "best friend" goes off with someone else, feelings are hurt and jealousy takes root.

Jealousy begins when a child feels that love (or something else) is being diminished for them when it is shared with someone else. They want the friend or the love or the attention back for themselves.

Feeling left out is a normal feeling, and the wise parent will try to understand the child's hurt. But if left unattended, jealousy can create additional problems—not only for others, but for the jealous child—such as sulking, withdrawing, suspicion, anger, or "getting even."

After reading the story of Pepper, Wolfie, and Goldie aloud to your child, you may want to use the following questions to discuss what causes jealous feelings and what can happen to a friendship:

1. How did Pepper feel when Wolfie raced with the new dog?

2. Why did she feel that way?

3. What did Pepper want Wolfie to do?

4. What did Wolfie want to do with Goldie? with Pepper?

5. Why did Pepper decide to stay inside the house and not go out to race at all?

6. How did Pepper feel when she spent all day in the house and wouldn't go out, even when Wolfie called for her?

7. Why did Pepper wish she lived in the middle yard (Wolfie's yard)?

8. Why did Pepper change her mind and go out to race with Wolfie after all?

9. What did she finally do instead of getting jealous when Wolfie raced with Goldie part of the time?

10. Do you think that was a good plan? Why do you think so?